I0531574

For Her

JIGO

Find your way...

September

Dear Karen,

I know you said that you didn't want to speak for a while so I'm hoping you'll forgive this transgression. In my defense, I wrote you a letter that, if you promise to read in your own voice, helps me keep my word.

I wanted to tell you a few things. I know this might be difficult for you to see (okay, I know you know this is a letter,) but I miss you. I still think about you every day. I wake up wondering if you're awake yet, if you can see the sunrise as well as I can from the room we used to share. When I daydream at work, it's less and less about what book I'm reading or movie I've just seen and more and more about you. Whenever I see something on TV or read an article in the news I can picture with perfect clarity what you would say about it. For a long time, I thought that I would have to change my route home from work. I still pass all the places we used to go together, but I've come to look forward to seeing them and relishing the nostalgic twinge in my chest.

The other thing I wanted to tell you is that I love you. I loved you from almost the very first moment that we met, even if that fact hid itself from my consciousness for a long time. I know I will love you for the rest of my life. This certainty drifts below my consciousness, giving me strength, and brings tears to my eyes when considered directly. I understand perfectly why we are apart and I don't want you to think that I want to undo what we chose to do together. I hate the fact that I drove us to this point and I hope you can use this time away from me to heal the pain that I've caused you. I only want you to be happy.

Lastly, I wanted you to know that I'm going away for a while. I always talked about taking a long trip on my bike, much to your understandable chagrin, and now seems like the perfect opportunity to take the time. I'm not running away from you or anything else here, but I feel the tug of the road in my soul and I know the time alone will go a long way towards the necessary healing process. The only reason I'm telling you this is so that you know where I am and what I'm doing. Some restlessly arrogant part of me wants to think that you will wonder where I am, but that might only be because of the amount of time I spend wondering where you are. I've told some others where I'm going and when I plan to be there with scheduled check-ins to hold me to my word. I don't want you to worry about me.

That's it. Wherever you are and whatever you are doing, I hope you are happy and well.

Love,

Oren

M1

Riding and contemplating make the world seem like a very large place. When you leave the urban noise of a city behind, the world is quiet and empty with nothing but the wind to fill the silences. More than anything, the man misses music. Out here in the open, even the crudest combination of melody and rhythm would be received as the clouds parting and heaven shining through.

The man has been on this road for as long as he can remember. The time has blurred into stretches of daylight filled by the rush of the wind and the thrum of the motor. Nights were deadly, quiet darkness accompanied only by memories louder than any wind shear could be. Memory had played a strange trick on him, making the road the only thing he saw when he peered into his foggy past. His heart was filled only with a desire to keep moving North. Finding the end was all that seemed to matter when he awoke each day, but he could not remember why it mattered.

The man didn't own much anymore but he was glad of this. It was nice to have a life free of clutter, giving his consciousness more room to focus on what was around him. He had been wearing the same well-worn pair of jeans, leather jacket, gloves, and riding boots for longer than would be socially acceptable in a world where things like that mattered. So far, the road had been kind enough to provide him ways to keep this second skin clean. His old Triumph certainly didn't complain, thumping, humming, and chortling, as it carried him along in mechanical serenity.

You'd be surprised how many road signs do not survive the end of days. The man uses the sun to guess that he is going north but in the end it remains a guess. Old farmhouses dot the landscape as far as he can see with little clusters of barns, silos, and farm equipment serving as their only company. A white house perched on top of a lonely hill just off the highway, paint peeling in the sun, seems like a good excuse to stop and stretch his legs. The man rolls off the throttle, letting the bike glide to a crunchy stop. The yard is filled with the remnants of a barbecue in full swing. It looks like all of the neighbors were in attendance, filling the tables and chairs scattered across the yard. The grill is open, beer bottles resting on its surface like birthday candles on a metal cake. The neighbors have been removed, with no signs of a struggle, as if time had stopped and they'd been erased one by one with the care of an artist touching up a sketch.

The house stands as still as a gravestone and the man does not bother to gather hope before he kicks the door open, shotgun at the ready. Just like every house he has passed this week, this one is painfully empty. The generous layer of dust covering the furniture lets him know that nobody has passed this way in quite a long time.

He takes a moment to stop and listen. There is something about the way the sound will reverberate in a room that will betray the presence of other bodies, but he can't feel any of that in this empty space. When he is sure this place is just a lost memory, he moves into the rooms and starts his routine search over again. The man has never wanted for supplies of any kind. His search feels more like a stroll through a museum that somebody has forgotten to clean. There are no attendants around in brightly colored blazers to tell him not to touch the displays. The house is a caricature of life, preserved for his viewing pleasure in layers of time.

The futon in the living room gives him pause. Despite a tangible layer of soot covering the entire room, the futon draws a familiar feeling from him. He struggles to place it in the emptiness that fills the miles behind him, but fails. Dust motes spin into the air as he plops down to rest. The mattress has a distinct sag, as if someone had laid in the same position over and over again. He swings his legs automatically to the side, coming to rest nestled perfectly in the sag of the mattress. The man must have had a futon just like this in the life that existed outside the smoky wall in his memory. Perhaps he'd even rested on one, just as he was doing now, with Her body next to his.

The man holds his breath as he turns the key on his old bike, but she proves herself once again as the most reliable thing he travels with. The sun hangs in the sky, shining its light on a day that seems to demand he acknowledge its idealistic beauty. The man can't shake the feeling that he's seen that futon before. Did he own one like it where he comes from? Did She? The road stretches on and the trees wave, inviting him forward.

You never think you'd miss people with their stink and noise and trodding on your shoes but the extended void of them will make you do it anyways. The man remembers the way he'd stare at people on the train or street and rain judgment down on them for their inadequate lifestyles. That was then. He couldn't imagine what could have made him so cynical, viewing the world through a pessimistic filter that allowed for no deviation from his design for people and surroundings. He found it frustrating that this part of his personality revealed itself with such clarity while others remained hidden. He thought he remembered what people looked like, what it felt like to have their lives all around him, swallowing him up in an envelope of humanity. Now that they were inexplicably gone, he wanted them back.

The only vestige of his former life that remains to him is this bike, but he would gladly trade it for the chance to talk to a person again. Any person, young or old, stupid or smart, would do. He still remembers the last person he saw before they dried up and blew away like leaves in the autumn sun. A little girl, in the back of an SUV. She waved to him as he passed on his bike. He was too busy thinking about how her parents were driving a big, unnecessary boat of a car to wave back.

The man used to read about the apocalypse. Zombies, nuclear war, running out of resources, financial collapse, you name it. All of them involved mass panic, violence, survival of the fittest, and a mad scrambling for resources.

None of them involved a disappearance, complete and endless. Sometimes it felt like he'd fallen asleep somewhere and that this world was just a dream that wouldn't quit. The emptiness and quietness were too perfect at times, lending it a sheen and glow that seemed to step out of reality. Countless times he'd found himself standing and staring at some innocuous object like a cup or a flower, wondering if it was real or some image his mind had constructed to fill the dream world he'd stumbled into.

The man digs into his memory for the hundredth or thousandth time for anything that might tell him where to go.

What was he was running from? Or towards? For the hundredth or thousandth time, all he can find is North. And Her.

K1

Oren turned the car into the parking lot of what must have been the tenth apartment complex that day. "Well, they've got tennis courts. That'll keep you entertained."

Karen nodded, undoing her seatbelt. "Yeah, but would you really play with me?" she asked. "I thought you hated tennis."

"I don't hate tennis," Oren answered. "I just don't want to play. It's not my thing."

"Yeah, I know."

Karen set off to what looked like the leasing office. Oren reached for her hand but she didn't seem to notice, pulling ahead of him. Karen was tall and slender and she moved with the grace of someone who'd had an active childhood. Her skinny limbs only hinted at the gangliness that she must have carried as a child, but her body had long since outgrown. Her long, dark hair flowed straight down her back, matching her hazel eyes perfectly.

"Don't look at my butt," Karen said as she pulled the door open.

"Can't a man gaze upon his lady's posterior in admiration?" Oren asked with a flourish.

"Yeah, but you're always creepy about it," Karen said. Oren only shook his head and smiled.

Oren could still remember the first time they'd met with perfect clarity. Well, the first time they'd talked, to be more accurate. Oren and Karen had been in the same classes since junior high. It wasn't until Karen had marched up and plopped down in front of him during a high school calculus class that he'd ever had a real conversation with her. One minute he'd been joking and laughing with his friends and the next she'd been there, just dropped out of nowhere. Back then, her hair had been shorter. Only down to her shoulders. Her eyes had still been just as deep, her smile and laugh just as full of alluring mirth. Oren hadn't had a chance, especially when the way they spoke to each other turned out to be so full of some magically addicting chemistry. Oren had never experienced what could rightly be called 'banter' before. He was a goner.

Oren and Karen positioned themselves across from the tired apartment agent. He always made an effort to look polite and interested as the agents moved through their spiels, but he always found his mind wandering. Karen will ask the important questions anyways. All Oren could think about was how great it would be to have his own place. How was one to live a normal social life when home was still the same one you grew up in? Adhering to a dinner time and sleeping between walls adorned with childhood artwork was not exactly the glamorous, post-graduation lifestyle that Oren had imagined. He had a new job, a new girlfriend, and he was ready to start his new life.

He sometimes had difficulty shaking off the restlessness that bounced around inside him. He often caught himself staring blankly out a window, not knowing how long he'd been drifting. His life had always been fun and easy and he didn't regret any choices he'd made to get here. This untargeted yearning was hard to shake, though. He knew he came off as impatient. He'd always imagine he was somewhere else, riding his motorcycle down a long, empty road in the sunshine with nothing to burden his mind except the wind in his face and a twisted throttle hand.

Karen gently nudged him back to reality. "This one looks perfect, right? It's a one bedroom, not too expensive, and I'll be living right down the street. Let's go see it."

Oren nodded in agreement, glad to have something to do. This time he caught Karen's hand on the way back to the car.

Oren plunked his end of the futon down with a sigh of relief. "Well, at least we have a place to sit now."

"And sit we shall," Karen replied. "Where's the rest of your furniture?"

"Still at home, I think. Mom and Dad have a storage space but I still think most of the stuff lives in Mom's collection piles somewhere." Oren plopped down beside her and the sag in the mattress rolled them together.

Oren eyed the clutter left over from the long moving day. "I've got to get this place cleaned up before my parents come tomorrow. I've only been here half a day, I can't look like a slob already. Mom will probably insist on cleaning every inch of the kitchen just for starters."

"Don't say anything bad about your Mom. She's so nice, I really like her."

"She likes you too, don't worry..."

Karen shifted a little, resting her arm across Oren's. "So she likes me?" she asked.

Karen's analytical mind was in high gear. She always seemed to be breaking everything down, looking for weaknesses and pointing them out. He definitely appreciated that she was logical. In fact, he relied on it. Sometimes he wished she would just be proud of him and what he was doing rather than letting the criticisms stack up.

Oren nodded impatiently. "Yes, yes, like I've said before. My Mom really likes you and she always has."

"Ok fine," she said. "She is your Mom, after all. That's a good thing."

Oren nodded absentmindedly. "Did you know that I slept on this futon for an entire semester in college? Pretty brutal."

"Is that why it sags?" Karen chuckled. "Freshmen fifteen come on a little strong?"

"I'll have you know I was a fine physical specimen! And I sleep like a log. Really, no rolling. It's kind of unfair to call it sleep, really. More like a coma."

"Yeah, I bet so," Karen said in a low voice. "Tell me more about that physical specimen."

"Well," he said, "I was just coming out of high school football and I still worked out a lot, mostly because I was-"

Karen was suddenly straddling him, stealing the rest of

this thought with her weight and smell.

"-bored a lot," he finished. She smiled and kissed him on the mouth, finally completing the true thought Oren had been having all day. Oren ran his hand through her hair, his mind dancing down the curve of her back with his fingers leading the way.

Oren couldn't remember anything smelling as inviting as Karen did. When they first met, he was immediately attracted to her smile, the way she cared about others, and her sense of humor that was eerily similar to his. Something about the way she smelled, though, made him think it could be a scent worth drowning in. It was always the first thing that came to mind whenever he thought about her.

Their clothes flew off to decorate the floor. Karen's body moved gracefully, waltzing with his to a melody that only they could hear. The rest of the world became an audience in the backdrop to every little sound that escaped her lips. Oren felt like they were on stage together in a grand theater, but all the seats were empty and the lights were out. Only the stage spots were on, isolating them at the center.

At the end, they laid together in sweaty contentment. Oren thought that this was probably the best way to spend time that the world had ever suggested to him.

"Well," he sighed, "the futon certainly never saw that coming. Had a strange day, this futon has."

Karen giggled. "Mmmhm..."

"Been uprooted from its home, strapped to a car, manhandled up some stairs, and then made to endure our sweatiness."

"Your sweatiness," Karen laughed. "On that note, I'm going to clean up." Karen got up and crossed to the bathroom. "Don't look at my butt," she said as she rounded the corner.

"Yeah, yeah." The light from the bathroom spilled around the room and Oren lay listening to the water, imagining his life here. Some more furniture would do nicely. This had to be what he'd been searching for, right? He had everything that a person could possibly ask for. As long as Karen was with him, he figured the mundanities of everyday life would just sort themselves out.

He hopped up and traced Karen's path to the bathroom and wrapped his arms around her.

"I see you're back," she said.

"And I see yours, which might have something to do with it," Oren replied.

"Seriously, my butt again?" she complained, but her kiss swallowed up any seriousness. Karen's skin was on fire under his fingers, her hair sticking to his chest.

They sprawled out on the floor together, happily spread eagled. Oren found Karen's hand and took hold. The sun had gone down outside, leaving them in a warm darkness. Oren could hear Karen breathing and for a while he listened to her, matching his own rhythm to hers.

"Well, guess I'm going to have to clean the Karen's backside-shaped smudge off the mirror before my parents come over tomorrow."

She rolled over and punched him in the arm, giggling madly.

October

Dear Karen,

I wish you could see where I am. I picked the longest, most lonely road I could find, but it's beautiful, in its own way.

I forgot how noisy cities can be. When you're constantly surrounded by the soundtrack of humanity, I think it can crowd out your own thoughts, blinding you to yourself. Out here where it's quiet, it took me some time to adjust to how loud my voice sounded in my own head. It suddenly had all this room to fill and it bounced around my skull and spilled out of my ears to fill the land around me. When you have nobody around to talk to, you talk to yourself. I know I sound like a crazy person but it's quite amazing what you can learn from yourself when you have the time to listen.

What I've learned is that not only did the bustle of our lives blind me to myself but it blinded me to you, as well. I was caught up in setting up my life, enacting the programmed steps, and filling the role that I thought society was defining for me. I couldn't see the effect that my waning attention was having on you. I know now that you were trying to reach out to me, to find me in the chaos, but I was too occupied to notice it. Have you ever felt like that? This realization is very important to me. You deserve someone who is not so easily buried in the detritus of life. You deserve someone who can cut through the maelstrom and connect his life to yours. I hope that my time out here teaches me how to listen to not only myself, but to those around me.

Do you remember the times we used to walk in the park together? On those walks, we'd always discuss things like where we wanted to go and who we wanted to be. You would always tell me things that were important to you as a person, that defined who you were. All I could ever think about was how your plans and dreams affected me or what I would have to do accommodate them. You were telling me who you were and I wasn't even listening.

Sometimes I feel like there is some part of me that's missing. I don't know if it's something that's buried or if it's something that I lack entirely. I think that I'm out here to find that part of me and reconnect it to myself. When I concentrate on that, it feels like I'm pulling apart the pieces of myself and analyzing them one by one. I wonder if shutting out the world with such intense introspection might be dangerous, that I could lose my way back. But right now it's therapeutic.

I don't want you to think that I expect you to answer any of these letters. I'm just thinking about you and this letter is a manifestation of that. Wherever you are and whatever you are doing, I hope that you are happy and well.

Love,

Oren

M2

The man strongly believes that all bikes have a personality. Some of them are plastic and robotic. Others are rumbly and old and some are classically wise. All bikes shake and roll to their own tune, burbling their stories out through the tailpipe for all to hear.

This motorbike had been with the man as far back into the mists of his memory that he could stretch. She had the most delightful way of prancing down the road, throwing classic style around with aplomb. She would have a thing or two to say about how the world should be seen if you could interpret the thumps coming from the motor.

The man shifts up into high gear, rolling the throttle open for a little addicting burst of acceleration. He wishes the landscape would shift as easily and happily as the gearbox in this old Triumph. The stubborn flatness of the land perseveres in every direction, broken only by what could either be distant trees or tricks of the glare.

The echo of the engine seems to take on a life of its own,

jumping away from him to dance and roll across the land around him. It climbs up and down the trees, bounds over the empty houses and barns, and stalks through the imperceptible valleys.

The echo almost seems to split in two, as if it has a friend returning its call… wait. The man snaps his head down to check his mirrors. That echo was definitely distinct, not something made by his bike. He had spent so much time listening to the his bike thrum out conversations with the wind that he'd recognize her growl anywhere, like the voice of an old friend through the fog. He slows the bike, squinting hard into the mirrors but he can't spot anyone following him. The road stretches back behind him in a long, endless black line. He can't see another vehicle between here and the horizon.

Sometimes it seems like the only thing that moves are the white lane lines rushing towards him in a perfect, rhythmic onslaught. Nothing around him breaks the hypnotic motion of their attack. Now, though, he can't shake the feeling that the whole world is watching him rush past. He can't seem to pin down what it's thinking anymore. The backdrop has suddenly abandoned its serenity for a guardedness that he can't pierce, like it's hiding something from him.

The bike flashes her fuel warning light jovially, jerking the man away from this drift. This must be a major interstate, meaning that a gas station shouldn't be too far off. The fuel light blinks away, hoping the man is right as much as he does. He shakes his head, glad to have something to take his attention away from the suddenly incoherent landscape rushing past him.

Sure enough, a pole with a broken sign on top looms over the horizon as a beacon to empty tanks. The man swerves onto the exit ramp, clacking down through the gears. The Triumph rolls to a stop in the shade of the awning. The gloom of the abandoned station is undisturbed by his arrival. When he kills the motor, the lonely silence drifts out to meet him, welcoming him to this quiet piece of the world.

The man tips the bike onto its stand and pulls his helmet and goggles off, savoring the feel of the breeze on his bare head. He pulls his gun from the makeshift holster at his side, swings his leg over, and makes for the gas station.

He barely glances at the pumps as they'll be useless without power. He's got to find the override to open the reservoir filling caps. With some luck, they won't be electronic and he won't have to blast them open. Shooting at a giant tank of flammable liquid seems like a bad idea. Finding some kind of release would be ideal as he had broken his crowbar prying at the last ones.

He weaves his way through the automobile husks, keeping an eye out for sudden movement. The cars are empty of life, intact or otherwise. Would somebody drive their car here for gas and then abandon it in perfect working order? His only answer are these lifeless hulks, left to rust and time.

Despite the broken glass, the man can't pierce the gloom that crouches inside the station. He stands and listens, hoping his patience will outlast any assailants. His gut tells him this cave hides no danger but he wants his senses to be just as satisfied. The darkness inside is heavy. It swallows the light from the sun, bending the fabric of the space around it like something dense resting on freshly made bedsheets.

The door creaks in protest as the man pushes it open and crunches into the store. A few seconds for his eyes to adjust reveal the station to be in the same condition he found the last one in. It's empty and as quiet as rest of the world and eerily intact. Nothing has been smashed, toppled, removed, or disturbed in any way. He checks for footprints in the dust, but can't find any. What power in this world disappears a populace so thoroughly as to leave their material world serenely unscathed?

He wanders quietly through the rows, kicking up the dirt in a slow, lazy cloud behind him. He keeps an eye on both the doors but this place is just as vacant as the house was. He searches the shelves for any useful items, mindlessly cataloging and comparing them even though he knows it's futile. His bike and pack are loaded with enough provisions for months and he isn't likely to find anything better in a gas station. He takes his time, hoping he'll find something more edible than aged candy bars and stale popcorn.

The man finds a skeleton key for the reservoir caps behind the counter. He hops up on the surface, dislodging a rack of gum, and kicks back for a smoke and a break in the shade.

The cigarette flares to life and trails smoke into the air in lethargic swirls. The day outside seems much brighter and clearer when viewed from inside this man made, concrete hole. Clouds slide silently past, the trees on the ground waving up at them. The endless blue sky smiles down on the world, oblivious to the man or any missing member of his species. If the man lets his eyes focus only on the world outside, the gloom in the station becomes true darkness. It surrounds him, like he's floating in space, looking in at the world through a window cut into the wall of reality.

The man wonders if She is out there somewhere, gazing up at the same blue expanse as he is. Is that why he feels the need to keep searching, to keep riding, to keep moving relentlessly north? Sometimes it feels like She is calling to him across the empty expanse in front of him, begging him to come home. He dwells on Her so much that sometimes She seems like the only real thing in the world. His only worry is that because She is so real to him, the idea of Her existing in a world that is so determinedly dreamlike is absurd.

He reaches absentmindedly for the novelty jewelry stand on the counter next to him and spins it idly, wondering if this is the same inventory the store opened with. The sun catches on the trinkets, making the stand sparkle like a lazy Christmas tree. His fingers catch on a simple silver chain with a brushed metal bird silhouette on the end. He turns it in his fingers, feeling the edges and the cool smoothness on his skin.

The sunlight catches it, flashing across his eyes for just

a moment, and suddenly the man is somewhere else. The glare is bright, making him squint, but he can just make out green hills and a fountain. He raises his arm to shield his eyes from the brightness, but it seems to come from everywhere at once. He feels a hand grip his and just as quickly as it started, it's over and he's back on the counter.

He drops to the floor with a crunch, rolls behind the counter, and pulls his shotgun up, panning around the room for his attacker. He holds his breath to listen but all he can hear the jingling of the necklaces on the rack. Dust dances in the light streaming in from outside but there is no other movement. A burn on his lips brings him back and he spits out the spent cigarette as he stands. Was the void around him finally swallowing his sanity as well?

He lowers his shotgun and rubs out the cigarette butt with his boot heel as he crunches towards the door. At the last minute he stops and backtracks. He lifts the bird necklace from the thin neck of the rack and slips it over his own.

Sunlight surrounds him as he steps back through the door. He breathes in the fresh air deeply, glad to be back outside. The volume of the world shoots back up as the sound of the wind rushes back in to fill the dreamy silence that thickened his mind in the station.

The man freezes a foot outside the door, staring back to where he parked. There are now two bikes leaning on their sides next to the pointless pumps instead of just one. They look like old friends standing casually together, waiting for him to come over and join their conversation. The man turns his head slowly from side to side, but he can't see anybody else outside the station.

"Let's see those hands, friend. Nice and slow," comes a voice from behind him.

The man raises his hands above his shoulders, not daring to turn around.

"That's it, pal. I'd like to keep this civilized. Now turn around slowly. Make sure I can see those hands the whole way."

He pivots to his left, making sure that his movements are liquid smooth. The man thinks that getting shot in the back would be a bad way to end his day.

In the doorway to the gas station, the same one he had just come through, stands a stranger he hasn't seen before. How this man could have parked his bike and gotten around behind him in the time he sat smoking is beyond him. The stranger is tall and solidly built. He's wearing a straw cowboy hat bent with age, and smoke trails up from a half-burned cigarette in his mouth, working with dark shades to hide the stranger's eyes.

"Who are you?" The man and the newcomer regard each other across the short distance between them, the stranger's gun never lowering from the man's chest.

"I'm Jigo," the stranger says. "I'd like to know why you were following me."

"I wasn't following you," the man replies. Something about the way the stranger speaks is familiar. It pokes at him through the cloudy wall in his mind, but he can't name the feeling and make it real.

"Well, seeing as we're the only two people here, I doubt I'm going to get a third opinion on that. Guess we've reached an impasse, friend."

Jigo stands looking at him for a moment and the man feels like the stranger knows something he isn't letting on. Something seemed to be right on the tip of his tongue. He looked like he was right on the edge of saying it when, finally, he lowers his gun.

"Seeing as we both appear to be here for the same reason, how about we work together and make this go a little faster? Seeing as you might be a member of an extremely endangered species, there doesn't seem to be much sense in shooting you just because I've never seen you before."

"Seems fair."

"Great. Let's see what we can do about getting this gas out of the ground."

Jigo walks past the man, over to where the bikes are parked. He moves with the lazy poise of an athlete conserving his energy, saving it all for the perfect moment. The man follows behind him, keeping a close eye on the stranger's hands and gun.

The man opens his pack and removes a small bucket with a skinny rope tied to the handle. He turns, seeing that Jigo has a very similar contraption.

Jigo chuckles. "Well, well, seems like have pretty similar ideas about the way the world works."

The man drops to his knees and uses the skeleton key to pop open the reservoir cap and gas fumes fill the air around them, their smell blocking out everything else.

"So what brings you to this particular stretch of road,

friend?" Jigo asks, unspooling the rope attached to his bucket.

"Just trying to get back north. This seemed to be the shortest route."

"Yeah, heard that before, considering it's what I'm doing too. I don't really know what I'm going to find to the north but it's the only thing I can think of to do on this empty planet."

The man nods his head, dumping his first small load of gas into the waiting bike. "Been out here long?" he asks.

"As long as I can remember, anyways. If you're going north too, we could ride together for a while. If you don't mind the company, that is. You're the first living soul I've seen in as long as I can remember. Seems like we'd better not waste whatever miracle of probability that just brought us to the same gas station in thousands of empty miles."

"Fine by me. It'll be hard to talk, but at least we won't be alone." The man caps the tank on his bike and starts rolling up the rope on his makeshift scoop.

Jigo nods. "I'll take lead first, we can switch whenever you'd like."

"Fine by me." The man swings his leg over the seat and

straps on his helmet. "As long as we're going north."

K2

"Man, this is one beautiful day," Oren said as he got out of the car, stretching and savoring the feel of the sun on his skin. "Feel that breeze? This would be a perfect day for a cruise on the old motorbike."

"You know I hate that thing," Karen replied, "I wish you'd never bought it. Every time you go buzzing up the street I just know that it's the last time I'm going to see you in one piece."

"I know, I know. You know I love it so let's not get into it again."

"Fine."

Karen came up beside him and slipped her hand into his. "Look at all the people out," she said. "Don't they have jobs?"

"Maybe they're off today. Enjoying the sunshine. It's what any sane person would be doing." Oren could see people running and sitting and strolling through the sun all over the park. "I still can't believe this park is this nice in an apartment complex. Pretty awesome, huh?"

"Sure is. Come on, let's roll. I only get an hour for lunch." Karen tugged him ahead and they joined the winding path, cutting through the bushes and over the soft hills.

Oren wished they didn't have to rush. He and Karen certainly had a different view about the role of the corporate world in their lives and nowhere was it more evident than in the time they spent together at lunch. His job just got in the way of the time he got to spend on his bike and with Karen. She definitely thought of her job as her life. He knew that Karen wanted to rule the business world with shining glory but he wished that she wasn't so intense on storming the beaches of working America.

They lapsed into silence, but Oren loved this silence. These were the moments he lived for, the ones that he spent his days at the office thinking about. Open road, no clouds, a breeze, and not a to-do list in sight with your girl beside you. Ruling the corporate world might be a worthy pursuit for some, but Oren just couldn't get his mind to align with that path.

Oren drifted back to the thought of the weekend cruise. If only he could convince Karen to come along, life would be perfect. He had his girl, but he wanted his bike. Surely

Karen could be convinced that the magic of two wheels outweighed the danger.

"What are you thinking about?" Karen asked.

"Ugh, that question."

"Humor me."

Oren pondered for a moment, watching some guys kick a soccer ball across the field.

"What do you want to do?"

"What do you mean, do?" Karen replied.

"I mean, do. With your life. What is your goal at the end?"

"Hmm.." Karen mused. "Well, I want to run my own company one day."

"Yeah? That's cool."

"But not before I go back to grad school to get my MBA."

"Grad school, huh? I didn't know you wanted to go back to school."

"Oh yes, definitely. I want to work for two to three years first though, get some experience under my belt."

"Of course," Oren said. They followed the curve of the path around, letting the sounds of nature wash over them. They crested one of the many gentle hills after an easy incline and came up on the park's crowning jewel, a fountain in the middle of a small lake. Oren could see the path winding off around the other edge, running underneath a leaning willow. The willow was keeping watch over a wooden bench, placed with a perfect view of the pond and fountain.

"It sounds like you have this pretty planned out," he said.

"Yeah I do, I think about this stuff. I like to know where my life is going, don't you?"

"Sure, but don't you like a little surprise now and then? Some spontaneity?

"Yes, but I also have some things I'd like to do before I settle down. Things I want to accomplish." Karen turned to look at him. "Don't you have some idea about where you'd like to be in five years?"

Oren thought for a moment, struggling with his answer. Of course he had a general outline of his future, but he thought in more broad strokes. Family, kids, financial stability. Karen's hard-lined plan worried him, but he couldn't exactly place his finger on why. All he wanted was to live life on the back of his motorcycle and ratcheting himself into Karen's plan didn't exactly fit with that lifestyle.

"I do, but I don't really like to plan. Life has a way of shaking all that up and doing its own thing. Two or three years doesn't seem like all that much in the grand scheme of things, but so much can change. You can't know where you're going to be or who you're going to be after that much time."

"Well okay, same question then," Karen said. "What is your goal? What do you want to do?"

Oren cracked a smile. "Well I know what I want but I haven't planned out the particulars yet. You're going to think it's really dumb."

"Try me," Karen said.

"Okay. I want to have a boat, not so big that it requires a crew, but big enough to live on comfortably. I want to sail that boat all over the world, putting in at different ports. On the boat I'd have two motorcycles. I'd get off and use them to, I don't know, just explore. See the world. Hopefully my lady would be the one using the other bike."

"Oh, your lady, huh?" Karen said sarcastically. "Have you replaced me, then? Hopefully this new lady actually likes motorcycles."

Oren chuckled. "Oh you know I wouldn't replace you, I'd just have to get an explorer buddy. We'd visit you, though. We'd just have to get you a nice little place near the water."

"Terrible," Karen said in exasperation, pushing him away. Oren wrapped his arm around her and pulled her back close to him.

"Joking. You're irreplaceable."

Karen slid her arm around his waist, adding her warmth to the sun's. Her smell crowded out the wild flowers, despite the bushes not three feet from their path.

They reached the bench under the willow and Oren sat down, holding out his arm for Karen to sit.

"What about a family?" Oren asked. "Don't you want kids?"

"Sure," Karen replied. "Probably in my early thirties. I want to be married for a while first, probably somewhere in my late twenties. Ideally I'd get married when I was twenty-seven or twenty-eight, which would give me plenty of time to enjoy my time with my husband before we had kids."

"That is really specific," Oren sighed. "I don't know why I'm resistant to the planning part so I guess I'll just let you handle that. Who needs it when I've got you?"

Karen moved a little closer to him and nestled into the crook of his body that his genetics seemed to have designed to fit her. He tried to sneak a look at her but all he could see was the top of her head. He settled for a deep inhale instead, pulling her scent into his nostrils. So what if their life plans were different, he thought. He supposed he could cite all that crap about opposites attracting but he really didn't believe in any of that vaguely astrological nonsense anyways. Oren believed in what he could feel beside him. Karen's warmth, the way she smelled, the sound of her voice when she said his name. All of those things easily overrode any differences they might see about how to plan their futures.

They sat together on the bench under the shade of the willow and watched the sun break and sparkle on the water's surface. The fountain lent a disruption to the water that somehow seemed to follow a set rhythm, rising and falling and gently crashing in a preordained pattern all its own. The muffled roar seemed to come from a long way off but covered the sounds of the park, leaving Oren and Karen in their private world on the bench.

The glare from the sun filled the cloudless sky, multiplied by its reflection off the water. He had to squint a little, but he could still see the green from the hills filling in the spaces behind the blue water. A formation of ducks cleared the tree line and landed gracefully on the surface, preening and shaking the water from their feathers, dunking their heads under one after the other.

Karen breathed in and out next to him. A content sound.

"I love birds," she said.

"I love you," Oren replied. She turned toward him and the look on her face convinced him that she felt the same way.

November

Dear K,

It's me. I think I'm lost. I found a road that seemed to call to me. It was a strange feeling. I blew past it the first time so all I got was a split-second glimpse. That's all it took for the road to burn itself into my mind, though. I had to turn around and go back.

Describing the way the road called to me is like trying to catch smoke with my fingers. I sat at the junction for a long time just staring down the endless miles. I knew logically that I could only see a few miles down the road, but it seemed to go on forever and just drop right over the horizon into oblivion. The ground under me seemed like it was at an angle, tilted specifically so that I would roll forward down that road. The world was making it easy for me.

I've been on that road for a long time. Miles and miles, by this point. Whenever I try to remember where I came from, this weird fog springs up in my mind, obscuring the path. This scared me so much at first that I made a regular exercise out of actively remembering why I was here. It was easy to pierce the barrier at first but now it's next to impossible. Now that fog is nearly impenetrable and I can barely see through it.

I'm holding on to the picture of you in my mind because I know thats why I'm here. I can remember your walk, the color of your hair, and the sound of your laugh. Most of all, I can remember your smell. It's the only thing I think about now. I have a hard time remembering what your face looks like and that scares me. That's how I knew I finally needed to pull over and admit that I was lost.

I may have lost sight of the path behind me but I know I'm not at the end. I know that I have to keep going. I can't really explain it but I have to find where this road leads. Even as I lose track of everything else in the world, that remains as clear as day.

I don't want you to think I'm crazy. I don't feel crazy. I keep thinking that what's happening to me is like something I have read in books over and over again. The endless monotony of this road has laid my mind open to the world, making it easy to project parts of myself onto the space around me and leaving me vulnerable to the power of the journey. The road is reconstructing me from the ground up, starting with my memories. I know I'm lost so I'm going to let this happen. The only thing I am holding onto is finding my way back to you.

Wherever you are and whatever you are doing, I hope that you are happy and well.

Love,

O

M3

The old motorbike carries the man down the road with absolutely no sense of urgency. Not even duty. The bike has reached a balanced pinnacle of purpose. His bike is carrying him with a perfect blend of speed and direction, reaching a mechanical oneness with the universe.

The man has come to envy the bike's unflappable ability to find this place. This mechanical thing was designed for a purpose that it can reach from the first turn of the key. Why is it that the man cannot remember his purpose? Did he know it once and simply forget it?

The man shifts his head to frame Jigo in his mirror. The vibration of the bike blurs the edges of the stranger and his bike, giving the image the hazy incoherences of a dream. Who was this stranger and what was his purpose? The man couldn't shake the feeling that he knew the stranger but he couldn't remember anybody named Jigo. Was he dangerous?

The bottom of the sun barely grazes the horizon, letting the man know it is time to camp. This lonely world could get cold at night. He eases on to the shoulder, checking his mirror to see that Jigo is doing the same. He raises his face shield so he can shout over the rumbling of the bikes.

"We should camp!" He points to the woods.

Jigo lifts his visor. "Yeah, getting dark! In the trees?" he shouts back.

"Yeah! Follow me, I've gotten pretty good at this!" He closes his shield and Jigo does the same.

The man picks the first opening in the trees and plunges the bike off the road. Not for the first time he thanks the forces that be for a bike that was designed with all around motorcycling in mind. He picks his track out as fast as he can, letting instinct and serendipity guide him through the rush of the trees. The Triumph really comes alive now, acting as an extension of his body language. He can feel every momentary loss of traction, feel every curve, and guide the wheels through every twist with tiny jaunts of his hips.

The man and his machine come skidding into a clearing in a hail of dust and rocks and leaves. Jigo comes sliding up next to him, sending rocks and sticks flying to bounce off the man.

"Damn, you are good at that, friend. I was sure I was going

to eat it more than a few times."

Their reckless dash through the wood should have awakened the world and brought it down on them but all he can hear is the bikes pinging themselves cool and Jigo crunching through the leaves and pine needles. Even the wind seems to have finished playing its song with the trees for the day.

"What do you think? Good spot?" the man asks.

"Looks fine to me, pal. Nice and flat, no sticks to poke me in the back while I'm trying to sleep."

"Great," the man says. "Why don't you gather some wood, I'm going to look for water."

The man leans the tired Triumph against a tree, sensing that it has already fallen asleep, nodding off as soon as he took out the key. He hopes he isn't far behind. He unstraps his gear, throwing it down in the clearing with a satisfying whump. Nothing like the quiet end to a long day's ride.

The man picks a direction he deems to be downhill and walks off into the forest. He takes only his trusty shotgun. He walks in a steadily increasing circle, keeping Jigo within earshot. The stranger certainly didn't seem to be hiding anything as he went cracking and stomping through the trees, whistling all the while. Perhaps the man could let his guard down a tiny bit. The man couldn't explain it, but Jigo didn't even feel the slightest bit dangerous. Vague familiarity was the only reading he could get.

After a short walk through the amber gloom, the man is rewarded with a small pool and a little waterfall, perfect for his first bath in recent memory.

The man lies floating on his back, watching the gentle fire in the sky intensify as the sun retreats from its day's work. He leans his head back, letting the water cover his ears, perfecting the soundlessness of his world. His heartbeat fills his ears with its slow and steady rhythm, letting him know he still lives. Surely he wouldn't have a heartbeat if this was a dream, right? Would his subconscious conjure up a heartbeat to make his dream more convincing?

His fire starts easily, crackling happily with its own existence. The steady warmth from the blaze presses on him, yet pulls his attention deeper into the center of the flame. Strange that he felt so alone before. The world suddenly seems crowded with all the bikes lying around and Jigo lounging opposite him, looking up at the twilight.

"Kind of strange that you're the first person I've seen in months," the man says. "What do you think happened to everybody?"

Jigo rolls over to look at the man through the fire. Shadow and light shift on his face, making his features dance.

"Good question, pal. I thought about that a lot in the beginning, but honestly it doesn't cross my mind much anymore."

"What do you think about, then?"

"This damned road and gettin' to the end of it. Seems like finding the end of it is the only thing in my head these days."

"I know what you mean."

The man shivers suddenly and huddles closer to the blaze. He looks around at his bike, and suddenly he chuckles at himself, thinking that he was about to bestow life on his old Triumph by asking it if it was cold. The bike really had taken on a life of her own in his mind.

"Do you miss people?" the man asks.

Jigo breathes in and out a few times and the man wonders if he has fallen asleep. "I think I miss them," he says suddenly. "But only because I was a part of something bigger than me. Now the whole world consists of me and that bike, bless her soul."

The man nods slowly, not looking up from the fire.

"People have a way of complicating things, you know? Half of them are stupid and the other half are so damned gloomy about the way their lives have turned out that I can't really get invested."

"Pretty bleak."

Jigo chuckles. "Yeah, heard that before." He sighs deeply. "Maybe I'm holding on to all the stupid gloominess until the herd shows back up to claim it."

The man wraps his arms around his knees and moves into the warmth, missing the soundtrack of crickets that he imagines usually accompanies such lonely camping scenes. The random pop and snap of the blaze fills the world around him, the flames occasionally tossing out a lone ember to dance its way through the night sky.

The man's eyelids sink lower, pulled down gently by his drowsiness. His view of the fire's dance splits and cascades into a cacophony of red and orange movement against the back of his eyelids. The warmth becomes a heat that surrounds his entire body.

Suddenly She is with him, the fire's warmth becoming

Hers in his arms. She spins and dances, standing out against the noise that fills the background. She swings and sways, Her head turning in time. Just as Her face comes around, the man jerks awake, kicking the logs in the fire. Thousands of ember dancers tumble forth, their frolicking replacing the fading image of Her dance in his mind.

"Shit, shit," the man says, stomping on a few embers that have landed near him.

"You alright?" Jigo asks sleepily.

"Fine. Just a dream, I think."

"About what?"

The man glances at where Jigo is laying. The stranger's hands are clasped behind his head and his eyes are closed. "I'm not sure, really. Somebody I lost, I think. I just get flashes of her every once in a while. That ever happen to you?"

"Mmhm," Jigo says. "I know I had someone special before I left. Mom, wife, sister, brother, uncle, who knows? I can only remember little things about before."

Jigo sighs before continuing in a dreamy voice. "This road running along underneath me has been like a big eraser, scraping away at my memory until it's all smeared and blurred on the page. For the longest time, I thought the road would never end. I dreamed that it would just keep going like some cheap funhouse trick."

"That's scary."

"Yep. Hell, I didn't even know I was going the right way until I met you at that gas station."

"What do you mean?"

Jigo takes a long time to answer. "Meeting you out here like I did seems… I don't know, right, somehow. I know I'm on the right track now."

The man doesn't know why, but he feels the same way. Jigo has voiced a feeling he'd been having a hard time pinning down. "I know I came out here to find something, but I've been out here so long I can't remember what it is."

"Yeah." Jigo shifts onto his side.

After a time, the man asks, "Who are you?"

Jigo chuckles softly. "You already know."

"Huh?" the man asks, looking up at Jigo, but the stranger is already snoring peacefully.

The man thinks his search must not be in vain. She was here, right here with him. He could almost feel Her skin, smell Her scent.

The man flops back onto the ground just as the first star heralds its appearance above him with a faint twinkle.

K3

"Alright, they're here." Oren clicked his phone off and slid it back into his pocket. The night scene had reached a fever pitch around them. The sky looked like a dark, smoky bowl plunked down to trap the muffled music, attention-seeking flashes of light and human white noise of the city.

The line for this particular hollowed-out dancing garage was already pretty long. Oren scanned the nameless copies across the street, but they were all the same. The undulating mass of people bobbed their heads together to the music that spilled out each time a door was opened.

Oren spotted the top of Jordan's head weaving its way through the crowd. The little space clear of humanity next to him must have been occupied by Carol.

"There they are," Oren said, already waving with comic enthusiasm.

"Mmhm, great," Karen mumbled from his side.

"Well, well, well, look who it is," Oren said, embracing his best friend. "Good thing you came out. I think we gave the city a respectable amount of time to prepare."

"Hey pal," Jordan replied, "Tonight, we will get silly."

"I've already warned the club that we brought our silly pants. They're expecting us."

Carol shook her head. "You two are ridiculous. Like overgrown man-children."

"I feel like we can't take them anywhere," Karen added as Jordan and Oren laughed goofily.

"But you just love us so much!" Jordan cried as he tried to pull Carol in for a big, mock kiss. Carol beat him off, smiling all the same.

Oren turned to smile at Karen, but she was already walking away, filling the gap in the moving line.

Oren closed the space and slid an arm around her. "What's wrong?"

"Nothing, don't worry about it," Karen replied.

"Oh come on, don't do that. What is it?"

Karen couldn't seem to look him in the eye. She bit her lip. "Oren, you always seem to have more fun with them than you do with me. If you don't want me here, I'll just go-"

Oren chuckled. "Come on, don't be like that. Of course I want you here."

Karen looked at him now. "Do you? Sometimes I can't

really tell. Saying it isn't enough." She pulled away from him and walked through the club door. Oren shrugged and went after her.

The noise and movement of the club was completely permeating. The low, red lights flashed in time with the music, turning the sea of people into the melody's fingers, toes, arms, and legs. The teeming swarm acted out its will, bobbing and swaying in organized servitude.

After a slew of drinks and shots at the crowded bar, Oren and Jordan leaned against the wall on the shore of the dancing sea. Oren could see Karen and Carol dancing and laughing just inside the breaking tide. Karen's smile was inviting, her joyous movement nearly impossible to resist. Oren took another sip of his drink, feeling the very first fuzzy grasp of intoxication.

"I'm going to ask Carol to marry me," Jordan said. "We're going on vacation next month and I'm going to ask her while we're in Venice."

"Holy crap, man, congratulations! That's incredible."

"Incredibly scary is more like it. I know she's the one, but it's still pretty scary to think about."

Oren nodded in agreement. "I know what you mean."

"I mean, this just makes it real. I'm a thirty-year-old child. I still laugh at farting sounds and things like silly pants. I know I want to spend the rest of my life with her, though."

"Maybe that's enough," Oren replied. "I'd be scared too but at least you'll be doing it together."

"So what about Karen?" Jordan asked after a time.

Oren turned his head to find her in the crowd. She was still dancing on the edge of the ocean of moving people, but moving farther and farther out. The rhythmic tide was pulling them out with its irresistible tug.

"Well, I love her. We have an amazing time together. She's my best friend."

"But...?"

Oren pondered for a moment, trying to find the words that described a tiny place in his psyche. It was one he didn't access directly all that much.

"I'm restless," he said finally. "I feel like I'm missing something. Something important. Problem is, I can't tell if it's a problem with her or something external. Sometimes I come home from work and I'm so impatient that I can't even stand to be around her but I don't know what I'm supposed to do to fix it."

"Hm," Jordan replied, swirling the drink in his hand. "You guys really seem to like each other. You're young, man. I remember feeling that way all the time. Still do, sometimes. Just don't rush."

In the crowd, Carol spotted them against the wall. She beckoned and waved, pointing them out to Karen.

"That's our cue, buddy." Jordan finished his drink and set it down.

"Right behind you." Oren placed his empty glass on the table and waded in, riding the current out to his lady.

Dancing with Karen felt like being on an island. The rhythm and noise of the ocean around them was constantly lapping at their shores but nothing could touch their world in the middle.

Karen spun and bobbed, her skin soaking up the energy of the red light as it bounced off her in the dark. Her movements spilled over into his dance and mixed with it. With his hands on her hips, he could feel his body responding to her swaying, pulling him deeper into the center of their island.

Oren caught the scent of her hair as she whipped her head

around, igniting the small flame within his chest. He felt as if the pace of the music around him was increasing, but he could hardly hear it for what it was anymore. It became like a red blanket that had been draped over every inch of their skin.

Suddenly the world was on fire around them. The red motion around them blended perfectly together, creating a backdrop of wavering heat. Oren could no longer see or hear anyone else but Karen. He held her pulsing body to his, moving and dipping together in a burning field of orange and red.

Karen moved her lips closer to Oren's ear and whispered, "I'm ready to go."

Oren snapped back to the world, the dancing mass of humanity coming back into focus. All that mattered now was finding a way out of this noise.

"Okay, let me find Jordan, tell him we're leaving." Karen crossed her arms and nodded.

Oren pushed his way through the crowd, looking around for his friends. He couldn't see them anywhere on the dance floor. He made his way to the edge of the crowd, scanning the bar for Jordan's profile.

"I can't find them anywhere. Do you see them?"

Karen shook her head. "They'll know we left."

"I can't just leave without telling them. I invited them out. Let's wait for five more minutes." Oren stood as tall as he could, but couldn't seem to spot his friend. The jumbled mass of humanity was moving too much and it was almost impossible to pick out individual faces.

"Oren, let's just leave! I'm ready to go," Karen said, frustration creeping into her voice.

"Alright, alright. Let's go." Oren took her hand and plowed his way through the storm towards the exit.

Back outside, the sounds of people laughing and shouting were almost serene compared to the press of the club. Karen moved in close to Oren's side. "I can't wait to get you home. I thought I was going to have to strip you down right there on that dance floor."

"Mmhm, yeah, me too." Oren was concentrating on moving them through the crowds as quickly as he could. Busy night scenes like this made him nervous and he had to focus on the task of navigating them through it safely.

As they rounded the corner, Karen suddenly stopped

short, pulling her hand out of his. Oren turned around in surprise.

"Do you not want me?" Karen asked, anger in her voice.

"Wait, what? What are you talking about?" Oren closed the gap between them in a few steps but Karen backed away slightly, shaking her head.

"I said I wanted to go. I thought we were having a moment and all you can think about is finding Jordan."

"Karen, what are you talking about? I wanted to leave just as badly as you did."

"Sure didn't seem like it," Karen replied shortly. "We wasted ten minutes looking for your friend."

Oren could only shake his head in disbelief. "Karen, of course I want you. I also didn't want to be rude to my friends. How would you have felt if they had just left without saying anything?"

"I would have understood, Oren! Why do you care so much what Jordan thinks? Sometimes it's so difficult to tell if really like me at all."

"Now you're being crazy, Karen. I love you, but I don't want to abandon my friends. Jordan is my best friend and I invited them out." Oren turned and walked to the car, shaking his head and muttering. He opened the door for Karen, then walked around to get in. After a few moments, Karen followed him, slamming the door as she plopped into the passenger seat.

Oren started up the car and pulled into traffic. "I love you, Karen, but I'm not going to be rude to my friends."

"Whatever," Karen replied, turning away to look out the window.

December

Hey You,

I feel like I'm floating. Not physically, like you would in water. I can see and hear and taste the world around me, but only in the way that you see faces in a dream. I am not experiencing it and it is not experiencing me. This isn't happening all the time. I know I'm awake because I feel pain and discomfort and I get hungry if I don't eat.

Believe it or not, I'm only just now starting to suspect that I'm losing my mind. On most days it seems like my head is so empty that there is room for the world to climb in and roll around a bit. It's almost like my mind hopped out of my skull to go for a walk and then lost its way home. I half expect to stumble on it one day, walking around in the broad daylight. I imagine it would say "Oh, there you are, old chap. I thought I'd lost you."

Have you ever been to a doctor's office and had to sit in the waiting room with all the other sick people? You know how sometimes it feels like that room is just outside the walls of the real world because everyone there is just waiting to be somewhere else? I've always thought the light in those rooms looks strange and that nothing sounds right. That room doesn't have an identity of its own because nobody in there actually wants to be there. That's how this road feels now. I know it's real, but I'm just moving down it on the way to somewhere else.

I wish I could remember your face. I strain my mind everyday with the finest sifter, but I cannot see it. I don't know who you are or what your name is, but I know that I knew your face once and that it's important to remember it. I see you in my dreams. I still can't make out your features, but I know it's you.

I don't know why I'm telling you these things. Maybe because everyone else is gone. I think it's funny that I would focus solely on finding one solitary person when the entirety of my race suddenly dries up like water in the desert. Do you ever wonder where everybody went? Are they there, with you, on the other side of the waiting room? I used to wonder that a lot in the beginning, even craving to stumble upon another person lost in the emptiness with me. Now all I think about is you.

Maybe finding you will help me traverse this waiting room world and make it back to the real one. The only thing I know for certain these days is this: I'm going to stay on this road until I get to the end. Something tells me that's where you are.

Wherever you are and whoever you are, I hope that you are happy and well.

Yours,

Me

M4

The tops of distant buildings poke over the edge of the horizon. The grey spires are taller than anything the man has seen in a long time and he has a hard time taking his eyes off of them. The monuments to his lost people rise up slowly before his eyes, unfazed by the emptiness around them. It's easy for the man to picture those towers full of people, floor upon floor, silently regarding his approach. The bike's tires spin the world underneath him, bringing the distant giants closer. The man can now make out the rest of the city sprouting around the towers like unkempt grass around the roots of trees.

More and more empty cars herald the approach of the city's border and the man tears his eyes away from the horizon to find his path through the maze of metal. He eases off the throttle and the rush of the wind outside his helmet is replaced with the motorbike's growling and snarling bouncing around the inside of the overpasses. The motorized symphony from the two bikes is the only thing he can hear besides the echo of the city's hollowed and delayed response. The stillness of the city is completely on him now, regarding his approach with a solemnity that the man cannot stop from creeping into his bones. The buildings all seem to turn towards them, leaning in for a better view of the intruders disturbing their quiet vigilance.

The man swings the bike around a gentle, high-banked curve onto a towering highway. The midair road stretches out in front of him, curving and rolling on its path through the buildings, merging and splitting to reach every small corner he can see, like flattened arteries tasked with supplying the city with a constant bloodstream of cars.

The scattered clumps of cars on the highway has evolved into a veritable blockade. Thousands of the rusty boxes stand in his way, forming a herd of wheeled sows, frozen mid-stampede. The cars have rolled and crunched into the dividers and guardrails as if the pilots were suddenly snatched away and they were left to come to a halt of their own making. The man weaves his way through the pack, careful not to disturb their resting places.

The man steers the bike onto a shoulder and a little room opens up in front of him. None of the lost animals have drifted this way. He pops the clutch and gives the bike a little throttle to chew on. Almost immediately the usual smoothness of the old Triumph gives way to an unhealthy jumbling, rattling his teeth and blurring his view in the mirrors. He can just make out Jigo's waving reflection.

The man pulls in the clutch and eases off the twisted throttle and the sound of tortured rubber are unmistakable as he glides to a halt. The man kicks down the stand, easing his bike onto her side.

Jigo walks up behind him, pulling off his helmet.

"Flat," the man says.

"Yep, looks that way. You couldn't have picked a better spot, though. Look." Jigo points up the road. "There's a bike dealership right up there. It's probably loaded with spare tires.

"Lucky me. I'm going to go look around, you coming?"

Jigo shakes his head. "No, you go on. I'm going shopping." He tilts his head towards the sad strip mall on the side of the highway.

"Right. See you back here in a little while."

Jigo waves a hand over his shoulder as he walks away.

The man rattles the locked doors of the dealership and

sighs to himself. Apparently the owners didn't even have time to open up shop before they were scooped up by oblivion and tossed into the void. He covers his eyes and peers inside, but he can't see anything out of the ordinary.

The man unslings his gun, pumping once to chamber a round. He aims down at the window and pulls the trigger. The resulting blast and shatter scream into the silence around him. After the last bit of glass tinkles to the ground, he can still hear the echo of the shot pin-balling through the spires around him as if they were passing word of his transgression down the line to each other. The man kicks the last of the glass out of the frame and crunches inside.

The man listens for signs that his egress has awoken anything lurking in the dark. All he can hear in the quiet is his own muffled breathing and the wind lazily drifting through the newly available pathway behind him. He walks the line of bikes on the showroom floor, his hand brushing each one and leaving a trail in the dust on their tanks. He bends down to investigate one of the tires more closely. The man thinks it'll probably be easier to take the entire rear wheel. A nice, easy swap. He stands up, looking for the door to the service garage.

The man freezes in place, willing every muscle in his body to absolute immobility. He can hear his heartbeat thumping loudly into the dusty stillness of the room as he inspects the reflection in the front window in his periphery.

Something is not right.

He can barely make out the edges of the door frame and counter in the ethereal projection on the window. The darkness in the doorway is framing another darkness and this one has the distinct appearance of a tall, thin person.

"Hey Jigo, done shopping already?"

No sound comes out of the gloom. He looks down at his hands, faking nonchalance. "Is that you?"

He takes a deep breath, fighting off the rising panic. Is he finally going crazy, falling into the bottomless void of the loneliness around him?

The man turns his head slowly, taking excruciating effort to move nothing else. The figure in the doorway materializes but makes no reaction to him. In the gloom he cannot make out the face of the visitor but the person is tall and slim, the smooth blend from head to shoulders indicating long hair. A woman? The man squints hard at her silhouette, trying desperately to pierce the shadow of the hallway. His panic subsides, replaced by creeping uneasiness. Why does she not greet him or come forward?

Steeling his resolve, the man turns the rest of his body toward the doorway, taking special care to keep his weapon pointed towards the floor. Once again, the shady outline makes no reaction to his movements. The man and the ghost contemplate each other silently across the short span of the abandoned dealership, the only movement comes from dust clouds reveling in the warmth of the sun streaming in through the glass.

The man decides he is going to talk to her. He opens his mouth to speak but can only shout in surprise as the figure turns and darts out of view, fleeing suddenly down the hallway. The man is so startled he can't move for a moment.

"Hey, wait!" he calls into the darkness. Another half beat passes and he sprints after her, dodging the showroom bikes and vaulting the counter. He pounds down the gloomy corridor, praying he doesn't trip in the darkness. The service garage at the end of the hall is lit only by the light coming in through an open door in the far corner. He slips in an old oil spill, pinwheeling for balance. He closes the distance to the door as fast as he can, weaving around disassembled bikes, sending loose bolts and wrenches clattering across the cold concrete.

The man crashes into the light of the outside, shielding his eyes to the glare and gazing around desperately. Was she real? He's in a narrow alley, lined with boxes and dumpsters and trash. Fire escapes hang down like metal vines from concrete trees to either side. The man scans every inch of the alley, but cannot see any sign of the ghost. He quiets his breathing, listening for footsteps.

A slight shift in the shadows on the wall ahead stands out like a flare in the stillness. The man takes off again, jumping over boxes and abandoned human detritus. He skids to a halt at the end of the alley and peers around the corner, trying to catch his breath. On the other side of the street is a tall hotel. A short flight of steps lead up to a grand, double-doored entryway framed by thick marble columns. The right half of the door is held ajar by the ghostly girl. She is turned back in his direction as if to see if he is following her. As soon as he spots her, she slips inside, allowing the door to swing gently closed.

The man jogs out of the alley, the wind tugging at him as he crosses the street. He looks up at the hotel. It isn't tall, maybe ten to fifteen stories. It's sandwiched between two nondescript office buildings, stretching up into the sky on either side. Deja vu seeps down the back of his neck. He's been here before. Stood in this very spot, looking up at this hotel in the same manner. This feeling, this memory, is even more powerful than what happened in the woods next to the fire. This moment had meaning he could feel with his waking senses. Instinctively, he turns to his right.

Jigo trots around the corner, sees him, and closes the distance.

"What's up? You look like you saw a ghost."

"Well, I did. Kind of. It looked liked a woman. I called out to her, but she ran off."

Jigo nods, almost as if he had been expecting this. "And she went where…?"

The man points at the hotel.

"Ah. So what are you standing around here for? Are you going after her?"

The man turns to the hotel. All of the windows are dark, like the building is trying to hide something.

He sighs and turns back to Jigo. "You coming this time?"

"You bet. It seems like you have all the fun anyways."

The man pulls open the heavy door, holding it so he and Jigo can slip inside. The only light inside comes from the doors behind him and the floor-to-ceiling windows to his left. Despite the brightness of the day, the light streaming in did not pierce the gloom further in than twenty or thirty feet. The man kneels in the entryway, setting down his shotgun and swinging his bag out in front of him. While he digs in his pack for his flashlight, he keeps his eyes on the shadows, watching for his ghost.

He stands after finding his torch and clicks it to life. The darkness retreats from his beam grudgingly, crowding backwards to make room for the new arc of light. To his left is a raised area with couches and chairs, huddled together in the dark in little groups. Their shadows look like crouching giants that move and sidle aside as he sweeps his light over them. To his right is a gift shop full of glass shelves holding touristy baubles that sparkle in the glare of his flashlight. Stare as he might, he could not pierce the wall of black in front of him.

"Damn, it's dark in here," Jigo says. "Kind of wish I'd waited outside now. You still going? Are you sure you want to know what's on the other side?"

The man nods in the blackness. "I have to see what's there. If She's there, I want to talk to Her."

"I know you do." Jigo sighs, as if gathering his courage.

The damp carpet swallows their footsteps as they carefully tread across the lobby. The walls are lined with cookie cutter landscape paintings and the fake trees and bushes that line the room cast shadows that spring up in moving caricatures of their plastic anchors. His light gives everything a colorless, black and white quality. He cannot shake the feeling of walking through a dream or a memory, his beam representing his mind's eye casting itself over a past experience.

The door to the stairwell stands open like a gaping cave mouth, the few visible steps leading up into an impenetrable blackness. He shines his flashlight upwards, but he cannot see the top of this stair-lined tower.

"What do you think is up there?" Jigo asks, his voice echoing up the hollow staircase.

"I don't know," the man replies.

"Well, I guess there's only one way to find out. Up you go."

Eight hundred and twelve. That is the number stamped onto the plaque on the door in front of him, the only thing adorning its surface. He does not remember his climb up the stairs and walk to this door in a normal way. It was not reason that guided his feet to this door, but something else. Something deep inside him that refused to be named or looked at directly.

Jigo leans on the wall next to him. "You ready to go in?"

The man shrugs, not taking his eyes off the number plate.

"I suppose that counts. You'd better go in there alone, I'll wait out here."

The man reaches out for the handle, fully expecting it to be locked. He is surprised when it does not resist him. He pushes the door open, using his weight for leverage.

The room is lit by a musty light filtering through the privacy curtains at the far end of the room. It's not much, but after the gloom of the hallway, the room is practically ablaze. The man clicks off his light as the door snicks shut behind him, closing him off from the hallway.

The man pushes the door to the bathroom open with a complaining creak that fills the stillness of the room. All the towels are perfectly folded and hung, the little bottles of soap and shampoo standing ready for the next guest.

He moves into the room, taking in the generic decorations, the desk topped with a pointless landline telephone, and the TV caked in enough dirt to smother the reflection in its dark screen. He moves between the two beds, perfectly made with sheets of cotton, blankets, and dust.

The memory of Her lying here wells up inside him to paint itself over his waking vision. He can see Her body giving form to the sheets, Her dark hair spilling out over the pillow in soft waves. He barely checks the instinct to reach out and touch Her cheek, his body jerking involuntarily.

He turns to the bed on his right and sits, throwing up dust around him in a sudden cloud. The man sets his pack on the floor so he can pivot and lay down facing the ceiling. His eyes drift closed as he swims in the memory that fills his head. He can almost hear the sheets rustle and the floor settle as She leaves Her bed. He moves his arms to the side automatically, making room for Her legs as She straddles him. He can feel the weight of Her on top of him, the bed groaning in acceptance of another charge.

The man opens his eyes so he can finally see Her face,

the one he left behind. The only thing he sees is his dust tumbling and whirling in lazy eddies in the yellow light between him and the ceiling.

The man steps back into the hallway, letting the door swing silently shut behind him. Jigo is now leaning against the opposite wall, one foot casually propped up against it.

"Find what you were looking for in there?"

"No, She wasn't here," the man sighs. "I don't know what I expected. I'm not even sure if I'm awake right now."

"At least you tried, that's the important part. Now you're closer to the truth."

The man looks up at the stranger standing across the hall from him. "How do you know?"

"Hell, I don't know. Not really, anyways. The look on your face, maybe? A feeling, more than anything else."

"Mm," the man nods.

"Look, are you sure you even know what you're chasing? Running down the ghosts in your mind can be dangerous. Sometimes they'll leap out of there and start walking around, talking to you. If you don't have a hold on yourself, you could lose it."

"I have to find Her."

Jigo chuckles, pushing himself up off the wall. "That's for damn sure. I'm with you, amigo. What else have I got to do?"

K4

Oren and Karen walked along the downtown street, hand-in-hand. The night was cool and clear. Oren looked up at the skyscrapers huddled around them, seeming to crowd them in, trapping him. He wished he were anywhere but here. "Remind me again why we're here?"

"Because I love this musical and you love me. Why, would you rather be somewhere else?" Karen looked over at Oren expectantly. Lately, Karen's questions always seemed to be tinged with a subtle uncertainty bordering on neediness. This was a new quirk that irritated him, like a paper cut in an inconvenient spot.

"Of course not," he replied. He pulled his hand out of hers, reaching for his phone. Oren turned it on to check the time for the fourth time in twenty minutes and struggled to suppress his impatience.

They walked along in silence for a few moments. Oren knew that he should reach out and take her hand again, but he couldn't bring himself to do it. Something inside his brain just couldn't get there, like the last firing on a synaptic checklist had been left off. Was he afraid to show this woman he cared for her? Vulnerability would make anybody nervous but this was Karen. He loved her. Oren could feel his exasperation with himself bubbling up, threatening to show on his face.

Maybe the problem wasn't internal. It shouldn't be this hard to connect. Maybe if it were somebody that wasn't Karen, it would be easier. More natural. He always felt like he was forcing the issue and the constant mental vigilance was starting to wear on him. He snuck a sideways look at her as if the answer to these questions would be written on the side of her head.

Karen caught him looking and tried to meet his eye. Oren quickly averted his gaze, pretending to be looking at a point over her head.

"What?"

"Hmm?" he replied, as if lost in thought.

"You were looking at me with this strange expression. What are you thinking about?" She moved closer to him, putting her arm around him and snuggling close.

"Oh, nothing," Oren replied. He made as if to pull away from her, almost involuntarily. This flinch did not go unnoticed.

"What? Why are you pulling away from me? Sometimes I feel like you don't even want to touch me. Like you're not even happy I'm here."

"Why would you think that? I am happy you're here."

"You could try showing it. Hold my hand, tell me I look nice."

"I do those things! And you do look nice."

"Oren, you only do those things when I ask you to or initiate them. The other night, I wore what you told me is your favorite dress and you know what you said? You said, 'Why are you so dressed up?' I wore it for you. I didn't have to."

Oren pondered for a few moments as they moved down the sidewalk in what now felt like a forced march. His frustration with this situation was now palpable, like a sour taste that he couldn't wash out of his mouth.

"Listen, you know I'm a pretty closed off guy. You did look good in that dress, but sometimes I don't know what to say."

"Are you shy?"

"No, it's not that. It's hard for me to say that stuff

sometimes."

"Oren, I need somebody who can be affectionate towards me. My father was a very caring and affectionate guy so that's what I'm used to. I want to feel like you love me."

"But I do!" Oren said, throwing up his hands. "You know I do, I've told you. How is that not enough?"

"It just isn't! You don't say it unless I do. You never show it physically. When I walk into your place, you don't even seem excited to see me. What am I supposed to think?"

"Karen, I'm sorry, but you know how I am. I spend a lot of time in my own head. I'm always happy you're around, but sometimes I just get stuck in there.

"I know you do. But I don't want to come over to just hang around while you're in your own head. It's unfair to me."

"I feel like I need a little space to think, Karen. Maybe a little space would help me."

"Alright," Karen sighed. "I can try that. But you have to try harder to act like my boyfriend. When people see us together, they could easily mistake us for friends."

Oren nodded. "I'll try."

They walked the last block to the theater quietly together, dodging groups of laughing friends and entwined couples.

Oren wanted to make this work, but could he? Had it been a mistake to push their friendship this far?

Karen's comment about looking like friends resonated with him. He sometimes did feel like he and Karen were just really good friends. They had very similar opinions and senses of humor. Hanging out with her was easy. They could talk for hours about anything, finishing each other's sentences and laughing whenever someone voiced something both of them had thought at the same moment. Maybe the reason Oren became so annoyed was that deep down, he didn't desire her as much as she did him. He felt that she was demanding too much sometimes and the frustration he felt now definitely corroborated that.

Every second that passed seemed to solidify this realization. It was almost an easy choice, as if the truth had been there in his mind just waiting until he shone a light on it. Maybe this was over.

In the cab on the way back to the hotel, Karen slid over next to him and leaned her head on his shoulder. The warm press of her body and the smell of her hair mixed together and fomented in his mind.

He definitely still desired her physically, but was it right to act on that now, after their conversation tonight? If Oren was going to end their relationship, it was wrong to lead her on. Now, however, the timing would be difficult. He had to find the proper moment to tell her about his decision, but he didn't want to hurt her or fight in the meantime.

Oren didn't notice they were back in their hotel room until the door shut behind him. "I'm going to have a quick shower before bed."

"Ok," Karen replied, setting her purse down on the table.

Oren turned on the hot water and let it cascade over his body, glad for a solitary moment to collect his thoughts. He knew the split with Karen was going to be tough because he did love her, despite his misgivings about their compatibility. He also didn't want to lose their friendship. Karen knew him better than anybody. She had always been there for him with advice and support whenever he needed her, even before they started their relationship.

Oren heard the door crack open. "Mind if I join you?" came Karen's voice, floating through the misty noise of the shower.

Crap. How was he supposed to say no? He also knew that

a part of him wanted to let her in. Karen was beautiful. The smell of her hair from the taxi ride wafted unbidden into his mind. "Not at all."

Karen pulled back the frosted glass door and stepped in, condensation already clinging to her body in all the right places.

"Hey."

One word was all it took to bring down all of Oren's carefully prepared defenses. He pulled her close to him, savoring they way her wet skin felt as it slid over his. He started at her shoulders and worked his way down, washing every inch of her with his hands. The water poured over them, forming little eddies and rivers on their bodies on its journey to the floor.

Oren forgot the doubts that he had been struggling with all evening. For a while, nothing mattered except rinsing off every bit of soap that he could find. Karen's lathered hands encouraged him, gliding up and down, transferring their warmth to his body.

In the drifting steam of the bathroom, everything was clean and simple. The heat washed away the last moments of their shower, but Oren wished he could stand there forever.

How can this not be right? Was it possible to be more content, more happy than this? Karen giggled as he put the towel on her head and ruffled her hair.

Oren stared up at the ceiling, listening to Karen breathing beside him. The warmth of the shower seemed like something from a past life. The passion was hollowed out, leaving room for all his doubts to come rushing back in. Karen was right next to him, but she already seemed to be drifting away. He seemed to be losing his grip on her, like the shower had made her so slippery that his memory would not hold on.

Karen murmured and shifted, rolling on to him. She sat up and the bed creaked in the quiet as she wriggled her hips on to his. Oren opened his eyes to look at Karen's face, but he couldn't see her in the darkness.

November

Dear Oren,

Thank you for your letters. I know I said that I didn't want to talk to you for a while, but I'm really glad that you wrote to me. I think I needed it. It kept me connected to you and gave me something to look forward to. For a long time I didn't open the first letter. I don't know why I did that. I wasn't trying to punish you, I think I just wanted to maintain my control over the situation. And yes, I promise that I read it in my own voice.

I want you to know that I miss you too. I think what we had together was incredibly special. Most people will go their whole lives without meeting someone they connect with as closely as we did. When I think about the way our conversations would drag on into the night and time would fly by, I find it really difficult to believe that we don't belong together. I can't count the number of times that I've found myself answering a question in my head, but in your voice. I know exactly what you would say and how you would say it. You're so far away yet you're still the voice in my head, always making me laugh.

I want you to know that you hurt me very deeply. I gave

everything that I was to you, so much so that I got lost in you. I tried really hard to be what you wanted in a girlfriend. You told me all the time that I was the best girlfriend you'd had, but some part of me always knew that wasn't true. Instead of accepting it, I fought against it. I had a hard time convincing myself that it wasn't something that was wrong with me. I think it was something created by our incompatibility. I still love you, Oren, but I'm not sure what that means for us. I definitely want to repair our friendship, but I think that I still need more time.

I'm really glad that you decided to write to me, but what you're saying is starting to worry me. You sound like you're becoming disconnected from not just me, but everything else. Even though I'm not there and I can't see your face, I can feel you drifting away from me. I worry about you out there on that dangerous machine with nobody to watch over you. I don't know where you are, but I want you to come home. I'm not sure what we'll be when you get here. All I know is this gut feeling I have is warning me that you'll be in danger if you don't come back.

Please come home as soon as you can. I'll be waiting for you here.

Love,

Karen

M5

The walk back to the injured bike is a long one. His body feels like it's struggling against him, wading through an invisible molasses that is hanging in the air. His consciousness is fighting to decide which universe to occupy. The man shakes his head several times, trying to force his mind to decide what is real.

The man turns to look at the hotel over his shoulder, but he isn't sure he can distinguish it from its grey companions anymore. The girl seemed to be leading him to that place, suddenly plunging a stirrer into the coffee cup of his memories. Did she know him and why he was here? Did she know Her?

Jigo turns to follow his gaze. "So, do you think you knew her?"

The man shakes his head. The more time he spent with Jigo, the more he was convinced that the stranger could read his mind. "I don't think so, but I can't be sure. Never got a good look at her."

"That's a shame. Maybe she didn't want to let you see her

yet. I wonder why she ran?"

"I don't know, maybe I scared her? Thing is, now I can't even remember chasing her with any certainty. It's fuzzy, like a radio station that's slightly out of tune. I can't decide if I was awake or if I dreamt the whole thing."

The man turns a corner into a hilly park and the hotel is lost to view. The deadly quiet of the park seems to swallow the sound of the world, covering them in silence so thick that he can feel it on his skin.

"I felt that way a lot, before I met you." Jigo kicks at the dust in front of him. "Like the whole world was covered in a thin blanket that I could just barely see through. I knew I was chasing something, but I was always afraid I'd catch it too, in a way."

The man turns to look at Jigo. "What do you mean?"

"I mean, sometimes we're so focused on ourselves that our mind shuts out the other stuff. That's why when you go digging around in your own head, you find a version of yourself you didn't know existed. Your ears still heard and your eyes still saw, even if you didn't."

"What does that have to do with the girl?"

"Hell, I don't know, kid. This is your story. Maybe all

the ghostly apparitions you surround yourself with are your mind trying to reconcile two versions of itself." Jigo chuckles. "Crap, I should write that down."

The bikes should be right where they left them on the other side of this park. He rolls the new tire beside him like a child with a hoop and a stick. The tire bounces over the fallen arms of trees beside him and the grass seems to crumble under his boots.

The trees thrust out of the tired ground like exposed finger bones locked in a permanent, painful convulsion. Though the man can feel the breeze at his back and playing about his ears, the trees seem loathe to move. The park is almost too still and suddenly the man regrets his choice of shortcuts.

Jigo pulls his leather jacket tighter around him. "Never seen such a cheerless park in all my days. Almost feels like a graveyard. You sure we couldn't have gone around?"

"Not anymore, I'm not."

The man bounces the tire to the crest of a small hill and the fullness of the empty park stretches out in front of him. He can see several small ponds nestled in the folds of the hills. Their perfect, silvery surfaces reflect only a hint of blue in the sunlight. The man half hopes to spot the shadow of a girl dancing between the trees, but is glad that her figure hasn't appeared to lend to the creeping uneasiness of the park.

The man grips the tire beside him, preparing to roll it down the hill. A distinct crunch behind him freezes his motions. He drops the tire and whirls, bring his gun to bear in one smooth motion.

Jigo lowers himself slowly beside the man, keeping his gun trained on the trees. "You heard that too, right?"

"Sure did."

Nothing stirs behind them, but that crunch definitely hadn't come from him or Jigo.

The stillness of the park deepens as if it is helping them watch for the intruder. The trees suddenly seem to crowd in around him, rattling their bony arms and blocking out the light from the sun. The world behind him contracts as if its being sucked slowly down a drain and he can almost feel the hill shift beneath him, tipping him back the way he came.

The uneasiness in the man's heart sparks and ignites into fear and he knows it's time to go. "Let's get out of here," he says, bending to pick up his tire.

The man shoves it down the hill and it quickly rolls away,

picking up speed and bouncing violently ahead. He comes stumbling down the hill after it, his pack clanking. Jigo crunches after him.

The tire has taken on a mind of its own, curving to follow the trough between two hills in front of him. The man makes the tire's path his own, following its bouncing trajectory over the grass and on to a concrete path half buried in grey leaves.

He matches the pace of the tire so he can alternate between shoving and running, the tire seeming to urge him on. He looks up and spots a narrow bridge ahead where the footpath spans a short river connecting two ponds. The bridge has handrails, but he'll have to be accurate so he doesn't topple the tire and lose it in the water.

The trees stretch and reach, moving in around him to block his path. Roots jump up out of the ground, making him stumble and stub his toes. He hits the beginning of the bridge perfectly, rolling the tire hard to conquer the short rise of the trellis. On the downside the tire picks up speed and gets away from him. He springs after it, but he's too slow. The tire catches in the small rut between wood and land and topples to the side, its wobble finally overcoming its forward momentum so that it thumps to the ground like a big, rubber coin. The tire seems to stare at him accusingly as he runs to its side.

"Better hurry, pal," Jigo says, coming up beside him. "I think this park is trying to evict us."

The man risks a look back along their flight path as he squats to lift the tire. If trees had a front side, they'd all be facing him now. The branches rattled and clacked as they slowly marched in pursuit. Night seemed to be following in their wake as if the last edge of the sun's shine was chasing them down.

Fear finds the man again and he raises the tire, giving it a mighty roll up the hill in front of him. He climbs the hill behind it, scrambling for purchase in the grass. He catches the tire and rolls it again so that it crests the hill and dips out of sight to begin its descent. The man reaches the top of the hill and a small pond fills his view.

"No!" he shouts into the void, but he knows it's too late. The tire is rolling madly towards the edge of the pond, the only things in its path a stooping willow tree and a broken park bench.

He dashes madly down the hill, his gait becoming a

stumbling fall. The man prays desperately that the tire will hit the bench or the tree.

"Shit, grab it!"

"Stop!"

The momentum of his pack finally overcomes him and he tips precariously. There is a final, panicked moment of arm-waving before he falls.

The ground rushes up to meet him and he barely has time to get his hands out before it hits him hard. He slides down the hill on his face, grass and dirt flying to fill his nose and eyes. He rolls once, the hump of his pack bouncing him slightly into the air. He is on his side long enough to see the gap between him and the bench closing rapidly.

The man catches a glimpse of Jigo, sliding down the hill after him. He has just enough time to roll onto his back before he slams into the bench's concrete base, knocking the breath

K5

It had been a month since Oren had seen Karen and the breakup was just starting to recede in his mind. The wound was closing up, the startling pain fading to a half-imagined ache. Seeing her get out of her car and stand waiting for him brought some of it back. The way she had cried, making him cry, razing his resolve to the ground and making the walk to the door ring with a shocking finality.

Oren had decided that he wanted to see Karen again. He knew that this relapse probably wasn't going to be healthy, but love has a funny way of overriding logic. Giving up your best friend wasn't exactly something that could be accomplished with one fell stroke. It was a bandage that had to be pulled off slowly.

He called her up and they decided to take a walk in the park. Open, neutral ground. Karen was waiting for him at the start of the path, arms crossed.

"Hey," he said, walking up to her.

"Hey," she replied, her voice all business. Oren wasn't sure what to say next.

"Well, shall we?" he asked with a little mock bow.

"Never serious, are you?" Karen asked with a tiny hint of fluster.

"You know me."

"Yes, I do."

They walked along for a while, heads down, Oren's hands stuffed in his pockets. This day could have been a mirror image of the last one they had spent here together. The sun was shining, unbroken by the cloudless sky. Despite the heat, the park was full of people. The ubiquitous soccer guys were sharing the field with a few frisbee players. Parents helped laughing children toss bread crumbs to the turtles under the narrow, wooden bridge. There were young couples and old couples, walking hand-in-hand or lounging on the grass.

"Lots of couples out today."

"There always are."

They lapsed back into silence. Oren started hoping this hadn't been a mistake. "So how are things? Everything alright at work?" he asked.

"Things are good, work is fine. No better, no worse."

"Well that's good," Oren said, watching a kite nose dive and tangle itself in a bush. The wrangler gave the string a few impatient tugs, solidifying the kite's grounding. "How are you doing after everything? You seem well."

Karen sighed, resigned. "Yes, I'm fine. I was really upset for a while. I had a hard time with it."

"Yeah?"

"Yeah. How are you?"

It was Oren's turn to sigh. "I'm fine. I had more of a heads up than you, I think that helped."

"You can just separate from it like that? It has only been a month."

Oren prided himself on his ability to deal with situations rationally. He was convinced he was better at it than most people. "I'm not completely over it, no. The hardest part for me is knowing that our friendship won't be the same now. You've always been there for me."

Karen sounded like she was straining to maintain her stern tone. Her voice softened and the words came slower. "It was hard for me, too. You were a big part of my life here. I spent all of my time with you, Oren. I hardly had time for anything else but I got stuck in this place where I didn't really want to be."

"Why do you say you were stuck?"

Karen paused. These words were harder but it sounded like this was the point she'd been waiting to get to. "Oren, I hated the version of myself that I was with you. I was anxious and clingy all the time. The worst part was, I knew I was doing it and it drove me crazy. I was so dependent on you and I didn't even realize it until we broke up."

It hurt to hear, but Oren knew she was right. "I think we were dependent on each other. I feel like our relationship crowded out everything else."

"I tried to give you the space you asked for, but it's hard when there are only two people in your universe."

Oren nodded. They started over the wooden bridge together and stopped in the middle to look out over the water. It was murky, but the top layers were just clear enough to see the turtles paddling in carefree circles, bobbing to the surface every so often in search of more breadcrumbs.

Karen waited for a family to pass before she spoke again. "Sometimes it seemed like there were two versions of you."

"What do you mean?"

"I don't know, exactly. Whenever we were out with your friends, you always seemed happy and bubbly. The life of the party. Whenever it was just us again, you'd close up and be gone to where I couldn't reach you. You'd get all surly and impatient. It was maddening. I always thought there was something wrong with me."

Oren knew he could be introspective. He'd been told he was quiet and introverted, but he'd never meant to be that way with Karen. He hated himself for making her feel that way. "There's nothing wrong with you. When I told you that you were the best girlfriend I'd ever had, I was telling the truth."

"I know. And it's ok, now. I've come to terms with that since we've been apart. It's just who you are."

Yes, Oren thought, and Karen deserved better. The ache in his chest deepened as he struggled to hold on to the blueprint of himself in his mind. One part of him desperately clung to the methodical, efficient persona he'd constructed for the world to see. His ego was wrapped up in it. Another part of him was already splintering, kicking and pushing away from somebody who could make Karen feel like that.

Oren looked up at the park bench under the willow as it came into view. The lake and the fountain looked exactly the same as he remembered them. The sun fell across the dancing water like a shattered crystal somehow still holding its light and the fountain joyously spewed the never-still water into the air, the tame roar reaching them over the sounds of the park.

"Do you want to sit for a while?"

"I guess."

They made their way to the bench, glad to have the shade from the willow to block the eager sun. The tree leaned in, like always, happy in its duties.

"The last time we sat here was much different, huh?" Oren mused.

"Yeah. Not so much space between us."

It had only been a month, but it seemed like a lifetime to Oren. Just being here with her felt so natural to him that he could hardly imagine getting up and leaving. Despite the time that had passed, this was the real fork in the road. Two distinct voices in his head argued over which way to turn. Listening to the part of him that so desperately wanted to stay on this bench would just lead to her getting hurt. In the end, he knew he had to leave. He had to carry this embattled creature as far away as he could.

The roar of the fountain sheltered them from the world, wrapping them up in its familiar blanket of isolation. This time, though, there was not one island but two.

"That should be the last of it." Oren handed Karen a box of her things that had taken up permanent residence in his place.

"Thanks."

Oren looked around at his apartment, thinking of all the memories here. Laughing, fighting, and that wonderful first night on the futon. Oren smiled to himself, savoring the melancholy taste of that memory.

"Well, I'm going to go." Karen said, breaking his reverie.

"You're leaving?"

"Yes. It's just really hard for me to be in here right now."

"I understand. It's weird how our conversations always seem to go on much longer than expected."

"Hmm, yeah. We're good friends, though. Lots in common."

Oren chewed on that for a moment. The question burst out of his mouth before he could do anything to silence it. "Do you think we'll ever end up together again?"

Karen shook her head. "It's too hard to answer that right now. I don't think so, though. I think we broke up for a reason. It was really hard to accept at first, but now that we're apart, it feels right. If we were supposed to be together, we would be."

Karen took a few steps towards the door, then stopped. "Listen, I think it's best if we don't speak for a while. This has been hard on me and I need some separation from you and the whole situation."

Oren looked at her face, trying, finally, to imagine his life without her.

"That's fine. I can do that."

After half a moment, Karen turned and walked to the door. "See ya."

Oren watched her leaving, wondering if he'd ever see her again. The door closed, shutting Her on the other side.

M5

out of him. The man sits up and shakes his head, desperately clinging to the vision. The tire lay forgotten beside him.

Who were those people? Was it him? The memory is slipping from his mind like mercury through his fingers. Jigo is crouched next to him.

"You alright, pal? You took a nasty spill." Jigo stands, looking down at him worriedly.

"Yeah, just give me a minute." Is this grey, dried world the real one or is he just trapped here, tortured with glimpses of the outside?

He stands slowly, bracing himself on the bench under the willow. He had definitely been here before. There was nothing special about this bench. It had a simple concrete base and a wooden frame with no cushions. He had probably seen hundreds of them in his life. Why should this one be special? The willow is lazily waving its branches above him as if trying to get him to understand something important.

As he stoops to retrieve the tire, he remembers that he had been running when he fell. "What was chasing us? Did you see anything?"

"Not a damned thing. I could have sworn something was after us, but it was gone as soon as you hit that bench. Weird, right?"

"Sure is," the man says, contemplating the tree-dotted hills behind them. Nothing moved in the grey stillness, despite the slight breeze. The park is solemnly quiet, watching to see what he'd do next.

The man rolls his tire onto the street and turns in the direction of the beached motorbike. After a quick change, he wanted to ride back here and stake the park out. He wants to try to catch a glimpse of what had been chasing him. The man knows he is secretly hoping for another glimpse of the ghostly figure from the hotel.

He knows that something has been guiding him here. It was no accident that he had been to that hotel, had walked through this park. The instinctual tug he has been feeling for weeks is gone, but he knows he isn't done yet. The end is in this city somewhere. He can feel its nearness like the faded memory of the smell of home. He'd start with the park, moving trees and all, and search this entire city until he found whatever would help him put this waking dream to rest.

"Well, that wasn't too bad," Jigo says as he stands, twirling a wrench in his fingers. "At least the designers had the good sense to make that pretty painless."

The man nods. "Not the first time I've had that thought."

"So what now?"

The man pauses for a moment. "This is going to sound strange, but I want to stake out that park. See if anything comes out after us."

"That is strange. What are you expecting to see?"

"Not sure, exactly. That's why I want to do it."

Jigo throws his leg over his bike. "Well I'm always up for a good stakeout. I just wish we had some coffee and donuts."

The tired bike coughs once, then growls contentedly as it comes to life. The bike seems to have a new spring in its step, a strut that can only come from a brand new pair of shoes.

The man steps the bike into gear and swings out into the road, pointing towards the husk-strewn exit ramp he'd trudged up with his tire an hour before. The light is quickly fading and he wants to set up at the park before the world is plunged into absolute blackness.

The concrete monoliths of the old city give way to more modest spires, allowing the setting sun to light his way. The city seems to have more color in the twilight, as if the world's saturation knobs were being slowly turned up in time with the sun's descent.

The grey husks of abandoned cars now have hints of metallic blue and dull red straining to breach the layers of rust and dirt. The man spots a tree in front of a small office park that has optimistically grey-green leaves adorning its ebony fingers. He almost wishes for the never ending openness of the country where there were no buildings to block the view of the sky when the sun sets it on fire. He remembers watching the stars pop out, one by one, in the inky black sky. After a day in the lifeless city, that place seemed like something from a childhood dream.

He swings onto the street running adjacent to the park and rolls forward. The bike's engine slows to a comforting gurgle as he scans for movement in the park on his left and the apartments on the right. Nothing stirs save a few brown leaves riding the wind and the shadows of the bikes following quietly behind them.

A quick turn into the apartment parking lot and it was easy enough to find a spot with a good view of the park exit. He rolls the old motorbike to a stop behind a convertible with a foot of leaves and dirt covering the interior. He and Jigo sit for a moment listening to the silence as it rushes in to fill the void left by the bike motors.

When nothing moves that the man can hear, he swings his leg over the bike and walks to a tree near the edge of the road. He slings his pack off, laying it behind what passes for bushes jutting out of the caked earth. He sits on the ground, leaning against the tree with his legs out, hoping the darkness will help him blend in and hide from whatever is lurking in the park. Jigo sits beside him and nods in satisfaction. "Perfect place for a stakeout."

This view is familiar. The lines of the trees and hills fall right where his eyes expect them to. Had the man sat here before, or walked in this direction? It was hard to tell in a twilight that turned everything into a silhouette. The park could have been the darkened backdrop of a stage, waiting for the actors to run out and start the first number.

Jigo lit up a cigarette beside him. The little flare illuminates the geometry of his face and the smoke trails away to join the darkness. "You know, I'm starting to think that the ghost you saw in the hotel was actually this person you're looking for."

"What makes you say that?" the man asks.

"I don't know, more of a feeling, really. I can see you dwelling on her everywhere we go. This emptiness does a strange thing to your mind, amigo. I'm not surprised the only person you ever think about suddenly appeared out of oblivion to lead you on a merry chase through the ruination of society. Hell, your imagination had to do something to fill the time."

"So you don't think she's real?"

"Oh I don't doubt she's real, man. I just think you'd better figure out if you're chasing the real her or the idea of her. The one that lives in your head. Best figure that out before you catch her."

The man nods, his eyes still on the park. Jigo is right, in a way. He thinks so much about how and where to find Her that he sometimes loses track of why he wanted to. Deep inside him was a hole that he knew he'd never fill until he found Her. It was made by Her. Ever since he entered the city, that deep place in him had been rising to the surface, making it harder and harder to ignore it. When the man had seen that ghost in the hotel, the emptiness inside him had responded, practically leaping out of him to lead the chase.

"Why did you decide to help me?" the man asks suddenly.

Jigo takes a long drag on his cigarette and lets it out slowly, contemplating the smoke as it drifts off into the twilit gloom. "When we saw each other standing in that gas station, there was this look on your face that I'll never forget. You looked like a cat that had seen itself in a mirror. Your eyes were full of distrust, but sprinkled in there was this surprised familiarity." Jigo sighs. "As time went on, I couldn't remember anything before I saw you standing there. It blew away, like smoke in the breeze. I tried to hold on to pieces of it for a while, but I couldn't. Seemed like your search was mine, after that."

The darkness seeps in around them as the shades of the world were slowly drawn. The world seems to settle, like a dog curling up into a ball to sleep. The wind calms too, its day's journey at an end. "Who are you?" the man asks.

Jigo chuckles as he drops his cigarette on the ground and rubs it out with his heel. "I told you, once. I'm Jigo."

"Wake up," someone whispers. The man's eyes snap open and he curses himself for drowsing. The world is quiet around him and dark as a cave. The light of the half moon above him is the only thing that allows him to distinguish the shadows of the trees from the dark roundness of the hills in the park.

The man whirls around to see Jigo leaning on his bike, smoking, and contemplating the apartment complex stretching out behind them.

"Did you see anybody?"

"Just you, amigo."

The man steps up, shaking his head. "Maybe I'm going nuts. What are you looking at?"

"Nothing in particular," Jigo answers. "I just had this weird feeling like we should go look around."

"In the dark? Could be dangerous."

"That it could, friend, that it could. You going to let that stop you?"

The man shoulders his pack, steeling his resolve. The wind had picked back up, blowing at his back. It seemed to urge him forward, gently pushing him into the apartments. He gives in, bringing his gun around and walking forward as quietly as possible.

Nothing stirs in the complex and nothing about it stands out. The tenants had definitely left in a hurry. There are very few cars left in the covered spots and some apartment doors stand open. The man steps carefully over a few exploded suitcases with their tails of scattered clothing and shoes.

Ahead of him, a mailbox has broken, the wind scattering its contents across the parking lot. Two cars have crashed into each other, their drivers not bothering to close the doors and try again despite the light damage. A small, pink tricycle lay on its side between them as if it was a prize the two machines had been wrestling for.

The man stops in front of a small building in the back corner of the lot. This building is unique in that it is smaller and only has two units with bigger balconies, as opposed to the four on the others. A quick scan around him reveals that all the complex doors around this corner are open, either left that way or kicked in, he can't tell. One door, however, is closed and untouched. The unit on the top floor of this small, unique building is the only one still closed to him. He squints at the wide windows on the balcony, but the curtains are drawn and he cannot see inside.

Jigo stops beside him to look up at the building. "So, is that the end?"

The man nods. "Can't be sure, but I think so."

"So, what happens next?"

The man turns to look at Jigo, but there's nobody beside him. He turns slowly, but Jigo is nowhere in sight. His surprise only lasts for a moment. In a way, the man had been expecting this. He had asked Jigo several times who he was and now he had his answer. It was just him now, here at the end.

The man trumps up the stairs and stops at the top, resting his hand on the knob. He takes a deep breath and turns the handle and the door swings silently inward.

Even if the man did not consciously remember this place, his body seemed to. His left arm stretches out automatically to find the light switch on the wall while his right arm extends to stop the rebounding door from hitting him on its return journey from an overly exuberant door jam. Though the light doesn't work, enough moonlight filters through the blinds to give the dim interior a faint glow.

The man's eyes adjust as he walks inside. A thin layer of dust covers everything as if trying to hide each object from his view. He walks to the blinds and turns them open fully, allowing the moon's light to stream in.

The man drops his pack on the coffee table. He plops down on the futon, blasting dust into the moonlit air to swirl in irritation. This was his home, he knew it. He had lived here. He had eaten food off this very table, watched his favorite movies on the television directly across from him, and laid on this very futon with Her.

He stands up suddenly, frustrated at the foggy barrier in his mind that is only letting memories through in small bursts. The familiar feeling of this place is stronger than anywhere he'd been, but it is still shallow and empty.

He stalks to the dining room and sifts through the mail on the table absently. Every moment he spends in this house lifts a weight from his mind. He no longer feels the pull of his journey, driving him inexorably forward. The emptiness of this place, despite its familiarity, is tinged with such an overwhelming sense of loss that it takes on a tangible feeling in his chest and throat. Here he is at the end and he only wants to see Her, to find out who She is.

The man sits at the table and places his head in his hands, willing himself to be calm and still. He deepens his breathing, listening closely to the sounds of the room. He is willing it to tell him a story. Gradually, the weight of the air in the room changes and he knows he isn't alone.

"You're here," She says from behind him. The small voice seems to come floating out of a dark past, drifting effortlessly through the resolute barrier that has been blocking this place from his view.

He raises his head, turning to Her. She is standing in the door, the moonlight dancing across Her beautiful face, lending its silvery life to Her own. She seems to have sprung directly out of his memory to stand here in front of him, smiling softly in the ethereal light. The radiance of that smile drags down the last stubborn bricks in his mind. Now that he sees Her standing here in front of him, the man marvels that he could have ever forgotten Her.

He stands and walks towards Her slowly, his body on edge, waiting for the moment when She would suddenly disappear, like Jigo, leaping back into his dreams. It didn't come.

Oren takes her in his arms, the familiar press of her body too much for him to handle. Tears stream freely down his face and he feels her body shuddering slightly as she cries with him. He breathes deeply, taking in the scent of her hair. Karen.

"I made it. I'm home."

Acknowledgments

I just want to take a moment to thank my wonderful first readers Cori Dombroski and Kendall Anderson. Their notes shed light on the darkest corners of this book and their patient dedication shed light on the darkest corners of me.

Though she might tire of hearing it by now, I want to say another thank you to Olga Vysochanskaya, the artist that brought Jigo to life in a way that I couldn't have possibly imagined.

And finally to my parents, I say thank you for being loving and supporting in the face of your eldest son taking up the arts. I love you both.

ABOUT THE AUTHOR

Chris G Barnes is a full time author living in Austin, Texas. He spends most of his time reading, riding his motorcycle, and ingesting clinically dangerous amounts of coffee. You can find him, and other fun things, at www.thisischrisbarnes.com

www.ingramcontent.com/pod-product-compliance
Lightning Source LLC
Chambersburg PA
CBHW060633130626
46555CB00002B/777